GO VIRAL

JEFF GOTTESFELD

red rhino
books®

Blackout	The Gift	Party of Four
Body Switch	**Going Viral**	Please Don't Tell
The Brothers	The Hero of	Racer
The Cat Whisperer	Crow's Crossing	Sky Watchers
Clan Castles	Home Planet	The Soldier
Clan Castles 2:	I Am Underdog	Space Trip
Upgrade Pack	Killer Flood	Standing by Emma
The Code	Little Miss Miss	Starstruck
Destiny's Dog	The Lost House	Stolen Treasure
Fight School	The Love Mints	Stones
Fish Boy	The Magic Stone	Too Many Dogs
Flyer	The New Kid	World's Ugliest Dog
The Forever Boy	One Amazing	Zombies!
The Garden Troll	Summer	Zuze and the Star
Ghost Mountain	Out of Gas	

www.sdlback.com

Copyright ©2018 by Saddleback Educational Publishing
All rights reserved. No part of this book may be reproduced in any form or by any means, electronic or mechanical, including photocopying, recording, scanning, or by any information storage and retrieval system, without the written permission of the publisher. SADDLEBACK EDUCATIONAL PUBLISHING and any associated logos are trademarks and/or registered trademarks of Saddleback Educational Publishing.

ISBN-13: 978-1-62250-983-6
ISBN-10: 1-62250-983-8
eBook: 978-1-63078-332-7

Printed in Malaysia

22 21 20 19 18   1 2 3 4 5

MEET THE

Annie

Age: 12

Favorite Dog Breed: St. Bernard (obvi)

Hobby: growing pilea peperomioides (Chinese money plant)

Dream Job: owning a flower farm

Best Quality: fun to be around

CHARACTERS

erin

Age: 12

Favorite Cat Breed: RagaMuffin

Secret Skill: knows lyrics to any song after hearing once

Greatest Fear: getting hit by a flying ball

Best Quality: goes with the flow

1
WE CAN DO THAT

Annie and Erin didn't look alike. Annie was short. She had red hair. Erin was tall and blonde. But they liked many of the same things. Ice cream. Big dogs. Annie had one named Spud. Fat cats. Erin had one named Candy.

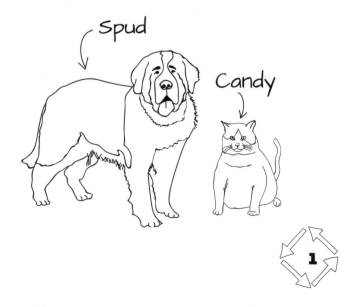

They lived in a little town on the same street. Both were in sixth grade. Their fave thing was viral videos. The girls were YouTube fans. They knew about all the video stars.

After school they would do homework. Then Annie would text Erin. "Hey! Want to come over and watch?"

Erin always texted back. "On my way!"

Annie would make popcorn. They'd hang out on her bed. It had fluffy pillows. Then they'd watch the videos. The girls would laugh and laugh.

Ready to go!

Their parents didn't approve. But what could they do? Tell them to stop? The girls got great grades. They played soccer. Listened to their parents. The only TV show they liked was *Big Don Tonight*. It was a talk show. Bands and big stars were on it. But the show came on too late to watch.

Their parents let them watch vids for one hour a day. The girls made the most of it.

It was a Tuesday in May. Erin was coming over. Annie made popcorn. Erin liked a ton of salt. Outside it was raining. It was a good day to hang out.

Their favorite star was Cory Mall. He posted new content on Tuesdays. Sometimes he did food dares with his friends. Other times he played trivia quizzes. He would do movie reviews too.

← THE Cory Mall

Annie was all set when Erin came to her room. Popcorn was made. Water was on ice. Her laptop was set. Spud was on the bed when Erin came in. He took up a lot of room.

"Ready to rock and roll," Annie told her. "I've got Cory's new one."

"How many views?" Erin asked.

Annie looked at the laptop screen. There was a number below the video. That was how many times it had been watched so far. "About 60 thousand."

"Wow! It went up today?"

Annie nodded. "It did."

"It must be cool to be Cory. He's such a star. I'd love to meet him."

"Me too," Annie said. "I wonder what he's like."

Annie patted the bed. Erin moved Spud to one side. Then she got on. Annie clicked play. Cory came on the screen. He was a big geek with thick glasses. He had dark hair and big eyes. He wore a Cory Mall T-shirt.

"Hi, hi, hi! It's me, Cory Mall! You know what day it is. It's new vid day! I got a great one for you guys. It's called, 'Cory Gets a Mani-Pedi!' Check it out!"

The new video was a snooze. Cory went to a nail place. He got his fingernails done first. Then his toenails were painted green. The staff joked with him. He teased someone with super long nails. They were filed to a point. It was not Cory's best work. Barely funny. Then it was over.

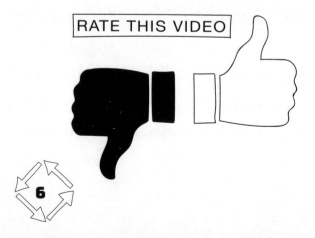

"Bye!" Cory said. "See you next week. I'll be on Big Don's talk show soon. Check me out! Buy my T-shirt."

That was it.

Annie looked at Erin. "Weak. I think he just wants to sell his shirts."

"I know. He can do better than that."

"Erin? *We* can do better than that."

"Stop it. No we can't. Let's watch more. What do you say, Spud?" Erin petted the dog. He barked with joy. "Let's watch a slime how-to. Fluffy slime looks cool."

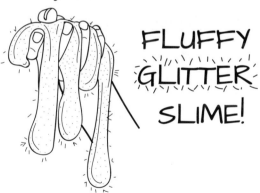

"No. I am *so* over slime." Annie got off the bed. She'd had an idea. When she got an idea, it was hard to let go. "We should try to do better than that."

"To make a video?"

"No. To go to Mars. Yes! To make a video. Don't you want to be as big as Cory?"

Erin made a face. "Ugh. No thanks. Kids make videos all the time. Most suck."

"Ours won't suck. It will be great. I'm a good writer. You're a great singer. We can figure it out."

...an unstoppable duo!

Annie was excited. What if they did get as big as Cory?

"Let's say I say okay." Erin rolled over to face her bestie. "We still have a problem."

"What's that?"

Erin turned her palms up. "No way will our parents let us. They barely let us watch YouTube. No Instagram. No Snapchat."

That was true. But what if they said yes? There was one way to find out.

2
TO BE A STAR

There was a picnic table in Annie's backyard. The girls got all four parents there. The parents liked each other. That was good. But this would still be hard.

Annie was a fine writer. Erin was a great talker. Annie wrote a speech for Erin. The girls practiced it a few times. Then they went outside.

They came prepared...

"Here's the thing," Erin said. "Annie and I want to try something. We want to make a video. For YouTube. A lot of kids do it. We'll have our own channel. It will be our own content. We'll write and perform. You can see it before we post. What do you think?"

It was a warm night. The adults had cold drinks. Annie's dad drank some soda. Then he held up his hand.

"Yeah, Dad?" Annie said.

"Why do you want to do this?"

Annie's mom spoke up. "I know why.

They want to be like Cory Hall. His videos go viral."

Annie faced her. "Mom, it's Cory *Mall*, not Hall. Like where you shop. But he's no store."

"I bet he makes a lot of money," Erin's dad said.

"From what?" asked Erin's mom.

"He must sell stuff," said Annie's dad.

Annie's mom grinned. "Not to us."

"He sells shirts. But we won't sell stuff," Annie said. "Okay. I'll admit it. It would be cool to be a star. I'd like that. Every kid would like that. But it won't happen. We're doing this for fun."

Pretty soon his face will be everywhere.

That was not all true. Annie knew it.

Erin turned to her mom. "Please, Mom? You like me to do new things. This is new."

Erin's mom even made her try fencing!

Erin's mom nodded. "It is. Give us a few minutes. Okay? We want to talk about it."

The girls went to Annie's room. They sat on her bed. Spud jumped up with them.

"What do you think?" Erin asked.

Annie shook her head. "I think they say no."

"I think so too. Want to check Cory's site?"

That's when Annie's cell sounded. It was a text.

"Who is it?" Erin asked.

"It's my dad. Are you ready for this?"

Erin nodded nervously.

It was not bad news. "Good luck, girls. Have fun."

3
WOOF AND MEOW

It was the next day. Erin had a great voice. Annie was pretty good. At least she could hit the notes. They would sing a song. But YouTube was filled with singers. They had to do something cool. Or silly. Better even than Cory. They needed to go viral.

Annie got it when she got home. Spud greeted her. He barked when she petted him near his ears. She petted him there some more. He barked again.

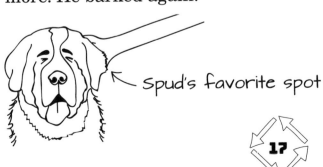
Spud's favorite spot

That was it!

She texted Erin. "I got it! Let's do it! Bring the cat."

Erin got there in record time. She had Candy the cat.

They went to the backyard. Spud jumped around excitedly.

Erin petted Candy's chin. The cat mewed. Annie wanted to use the pets in the video. She and Erin would sing. The animals would make sounds. It would be funny. At least she hoped so.

Annie set up her phone. She put it on a

stand. The picture was clear. The sound was good. They practiced a few times. The next one she recorded.

The song was simple. Some would call it lame. But could the animals pull it off? Annie was hoping for a few hits. Who did they think they were? Grumpy Cat?

Row, row, row your boat,
Gently down the stream.
Woof! Woof! Woof! Meow!
Life is but a dream.

The first three takes were bad. A plane

flew by. Then the dog burped. The phone froze. Annie got mad at herself. Now who did they think they were? Cory Mall? They were kids. This was silly.

This is too hard. We should just stick to watch parties.

"Just one more try," Annie said. She sighed.

"Will Spud burp more?"

"Gross. I hope not." Annie looked at Spud. He looked up at her. She knew that look. He wanted to go for a walk. They didn't have much time. "Okay. One more try."

She touched her phone. It started to record. Then she went to Erin. Candy was in Erin's arms. Annie put a hand on Spud. Erin sang. Annie joined in.

It worked! The dog barked. The cat mewed. They did four verses. Annie made the last one extra funny.

Row, row, row your boat,
Gently down the stream.
Meow! Meow!
If you see your evil twin,
Hope she isn't mean!
Woof! Woof!

Later, Annie plugged her phone into the laptop. She and Erin edited the video. They created their channel. There was an About section. They described themselves. The girls used their first names. A map showed their town. It was time. Annie was excited for their first post.

"Ready?" she asked.

"You know it!" Erin said.

Annie tapped her laptop.

It was a big moment. The video was up. She hoped it would go viral.

Here goes nothing...

4
OMG!

It was the next morning. Annie's alarm went off at seven. Her parents had been nice. They let her have her phone in the room. She reached for it. Then she clicked to the video. She wanted to see the counter. She hoped for lots of views.

Okay. At least 50.

But it wasn't 50.

It was six.

"Six!" she said out loud. "Ugh! We can do better than that."

The girls had each watched it three times. That meant no one else had seen it. Embarrassing. She was no star. Not even close.

She got out of bed. It was time for school. Erin's text came as she brushed her teeth. "We're not viral."

"I know," Annie said.

"We're not the next Cory Mall."

Just two nobodies.

"Nope," Annie said. "We bombed. See you at school. Don't forget soccer."

The girls were on the same team. Practice was after school.

School was fine. Annie checked online at lunch. The counter hadn't moved. Still just six hits.

They showed the video to some kids. Randa loved it. She shared it with some friends. Everyone laughed except Tommy. The boy was in glee club. He said the singing was good. But the pets were lame.

The bell rang as Annie and Erin walked to art class.

Erin LOVES art class.

Annie not so much.

"I'm done with this," Annie said.

Erin nodded. "Me too."

"Do we take it down? I want to take it down," Annie told her.

Erin shook her head. "No. Let's keep it online. To remind us."

"Of what?"

"Not to do it again!"

Annie grinned. "That's a good idea."

The rest of the day was okay. Annie did her work. Soccer was next. Annie dressed and ran to the field. She passed Tommy. He was with Randa.

This will help take our minds off the video...

"Hey look! It's the video star," Tommy called. "Where's Erin?"

Annie stopped. "She's changing. Don't be mean, Tommy. It's not nice."

"No, no," Randa said. "Tommy's not being mean. You two are big stars."

"Not funny," Annie told her.

"Yes it is," Randa said. "That's why there are so many views."

Annie felt her heart race. She tried to stay calm. "What's going on? And don't mess with me."

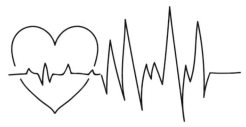

Randa held her cell phone. She gave it to Annie. "Look at your video."

There it was. Annie saw there were tons of views. She jumped for joy. "Yes! I need to tell Erin. Can I use your phone?"

Randa grinned. "Sure."

Girls were kicking balls around. The coach started drills. It was time to play.

But Annie had to share the news. She knew Erin's number. She sent a quick text. "It's me. We're viral!"

5
STARS

Erin stayed at Annie's. They did their homework first. But they kept looking at numbers. So did their parents.

The two families ate dinner together. More and more kids saw their video. People wrote nice things in the comments.

Pizza to celebrate!

"You girls are the best!"

"So much fun. Thanks!"

"I want your pets."

"Do more! Do more!"

Then came texts from kids at school. The best was from Tommy. "I goofed. You guys rock. Forgive me. Tell me if I can help."

"What do I say to him?" Annie asked.

"He said sorry. You have to say okay."

Annie texted back. "No prob. Will do. Thanks!"

Now there was work to do. The girls wanted a website. It would be a good place for news. Setup was easy. Erin wrote a note for their fans. Annie posted pics of the pets.

Fans wrote comments. The girls replied to them. More fans posted nice words. Some even linked to the song.

The parents were in the living room. They kept an eye on the girls. Annie's dad came in a lot. He seemed to enjoy the whole thing. "So, this is going viral?"

"Yes! This is going viral," Annie said. She was in a daze. So many kids tried to do what they did. Luck had been with them. They were a hit!

Annie's dad looked at the laptop. "Can you show a video by Cory—"

His cell rang. It was a call, not a text. He put it to his ear.

"Hello?" He listened for a bit. "How do I feel? I'm proud. You want to talk to the girls?" He held out the phone to Annie. "It's a reporter. She wants to talk to you guys. It's on speaker. She called you 'stars.'"

"Reporter?! What do I say?"

Annie gulped. Talk with a reporter? That was what real stars did.

The writer's name was Sue. It had been easy to find the girls. They had put their names and town online.

"I don't have much time," Sue said. "Just

two things. Did you have any idea you would be a hit?"

"None at all," Annie said. "We just did our best. And had fun."

"Got it. And what do you think of the haters?" Sue asked.

"The who?" Erin asked.

"The haters. The ones that hate your video."

"What haters?" Annie asked.

"Haven't you read all the comments?"

"No," Annie said. She felt a little sick at the idea of being hated on.

"Check them out," Sue said. "They're … not so nice."

Annie's dad got mad. "Come on, Sue. They're just kids. Why do you want them to feel bad?"

"Don't get mad at me, sir. I'm just doing my job," Sue shot back.

"I think we're done here." Annie's dad clicked off.

Annie didn't know what to do. Part of her wanted to see the mean comments. Part of her didn't. The part that wanted to see them won.

She read many of them. They were not just mean. They were nasty.

"You girls suck!"

"This bites!"

"Not funny. Lame."

"So super sad."

"Mean to the dog and cat."

"The pets sing best!"

When she'd read some, Erin turned to Annie. "Trolls. I wish they'd shut up."

Trolls hide behind their computers.

Annie nodded. "I know how to make that happen."

Erin tilted her head. "Tell me. I'm all ears."

Annie grinned and looked at her dad. "I want to make sure it's okay. Can we make a new one? Even better than this one. All right, Dad?"

6
ON A MISSION

It was the next day. There was no school. It gave Annie and Erin lots of time.

That's early for a Saturday!

First they called Tommy. He could be mean. But he could sing. Annie asked him to help. Tommy wanted to be a star. He was in. His parents had agreed.

Then they called Randa. She didn't sing.

Drums were her jam. She had mad skills. Annie had one question. Could she keep a beat on a box? Randa said sure. She didn't care what she hit. Give her two sticks. She'd be fine.

Annie planned the next song. The kids filmed it in her backyard. Her dad came to help. Annie had Spud. Erin had Candy.

All the kids wore white shirts and black pants. Annie wanted to do "This Little Light of Mine." Randa would keep time on the box. Tommy sang the low notes. Annie did the middle. Erin took the high ones. They tried it a few times with the pets. It was fine.

"Let's do it," Annie said. "Dad, start to film."

Her dad aimed the phone. They sang with all they had. The pets were at their best.

This little light of mine,
I'm gonna let it shine.
Woof! Meow!
This little light of mine,
I'm gonna let it shine.
Woof! Meow!
This little light of mine,
I'm gonna let it shine.
Let it shine,
Let it shine,
Let it shine.
Woof! Woof! Meow!

They all watched the tape. It rocked. They just had to post it.

Annie couldn't wait. She cupped her hands around her mouth. Then she yelled, "Take that, haters!"

7
THE CALL

The first video had been a hit. This one was a monster hit.

The day after, the girls tried to be normal. They took Spud for a walk. Candy got a new toy. They even watch some videos. Their numbers were good. But they didn't want to go nuts over it.

Candy's new toy

Erin and her parents came for dinner again. They had burgers. Annie's dad got out the laptop when they were done. "Ready?" he asked.

Annie's mom made strawberry milkshakes for dessert.

"Bring it," said Annie.

He pushed the laptop to her. "You guys made it. Check it out."

"We love you no matter what," Annie's mom said. "You're the same girls."

Annie smiled. That was such a mom thing to say. But it was true.

"Thanks, Mom."

Annie looked. Her jaw dropped. There were so many views! Far more than last time. And more comments. So many nice ones. Only a few haters. She didn't even mind them. It was easy to hate on someone doing good. It was a lot harder to *do* good.

The girls took the dog to Annie's room. They wrote on their website. They texted Tommy and Randa.

Erin and her parents finally went home. Annie got set for bed. She recalled her idea from dinner about doing good. It felt like a thing to live by. She even wrote it down on a file card.

> It's easy to hate on someone doing good. It's a lot harder to do good.

She snapped a picture of the words. Then she sent it to Erin. Erin texted back. "Yes! Post it on our site."

Annie did. When she was a true star, she wanted to do a lot of good.

Some causes Annie cares about:

"Annie? Annie?"

Annie opened her eyes. Her mom and dad stood over her. Wow. Had she slept too long? She looked at her clock. No. She was fine. It wasn't late. In fact, she had 30 more minutes. So why were they here?

"I'm awake. What?"

"Get dressed. You have a call to take. A video call."

"What are you talking about?" Annie rubbed her eyes. She loved to sleep. Her parents had robbed her.

"This better be good."

Her dad took her arm. "Just do it. You want to talk to him."

"Who?"

"We'll tell you when you come down," her mom said. "Brush your hair."

"It's good news, Annie," said her dad. "It's very good."

They left. Annie was in the kitchen with two minutes to spare. The laptop was on the table. It seemed to live there these days.

"How are our numbers?" she asked her dad.

"Huge."

"Who's calling me? Cory Mall?"

Her dad grinned. "Better. You'll see in a sec. It's a video call."

The laptop sounded with two tones. The call was coming in.

"Get in front of the computer," her dad said.

Annie did. Her dad clicked to start the call. A face filled the screen.

"Annie! Good morning. Hate to get you up. But that's show biz. How you doing? You're a big star!"

Oh my gosh! Annie knew the face right away. It was Big Don. She loved him so much. Then it hit her. He had seen the videos. That was why he was calling.

"You kids are the best," said Big Don. "Let me ask. Will you come to New York to be on my show? You and your friends? You have a name yet? If not, get one. You guys are the real deal. Not fake. Kids having fun. I love it. Just post one more video. I know you can do it. Your folks can call me. Let me know in an hour if you can come. Next week is good. Same show as Cory Mall. Okay? Bye."

The screen went dark. Annie was stunned.

Big Don wanted them on his TV show? On the same show as Cory Mall? No way.

Her mom smiled. "It's nice in New York in May."

Yes! She would be on TV. They would meet Cory Mall. Life was good.

8
ONE MORE VID

Big Don wanted one more. They did one more.

First they picked a name. Annie liked Just Some Kids. They added it to their channel. The world loved it.

The updated page!

Everything happened fast. The new video would be big. It would look slick and be shot by pros. Big Don paid for the film crew. He paid for a stage in a big park. There was good lighting.

We felt like real professionals!

It was the day of the show. Crowds came to watch. They'd heard about it on the radio. Big Don invited sick kids from the hospital. There were seats for them in front.

Annie and Erin met the kids. There were lots of hugs. It felt good.

At last it was time to sing. They had a new song. Annie's dad ran the show. He got the crowd revved up. "Okay! Here are the ones you want. The ones the world wants. Give it up! It's Just Some Kids!"

The kids and pets came out. They had a new song to do. It was a song no one could hate.

I'd like to teach the world to sing
Woof! Woof! Woof! Meow!
In perfect harmony
Woof! Woof! Woof! Meow!

The crew filmed. The crowd danced. Annie felt a tear in her eye. This was so much fun. It made people feel good. It was like what she wrote on the file card. This was doing good.

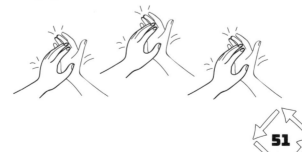

The kids did all three of their songs. Then the show was over. There were huge cheers. It felt like a sure thing. Randa and Tommy high-fived. Erin squeezed Candy.

Annie was set to be bigger than ever. She could feel it.

9
FAIL!

The video went up late on Sunday. The numbers were the best yet. Annie started to plan for New York. All four kids would go. Parents too. And the pets. It would be a crazy flight.

Would there be enough time to see the sights? Annie hoped so. There was a lot she wanted to do. Would Cory want to go to lunch with them? That would be sweet!

We could go get pho. (Cory's favorite)

She'd read about Big Don's show. They would do two songs, she hoped. Her only worry was if the pets got sick. That would be bad. Oh well. What could they do about it? Not much.

The next day was school. Her alarm went off at 6:45. She checked the numbers. Still strong. She washed and dressed. Breakfast was always with her folks.

Her mom was a nurse. The hours always changed. Her dad ran an office. He would drive her to school.

She ran down to eat. "So, ready for …"

Mom has not touched her tea or gluten-free waffles.

Uh-oh. Something was wrong. Her mom wasn't eating. Her dad stared at his coffee. No one spoke.

"What's the matter?" Annie asked.

She sat down. There was only one thing that could be wrong. The video.

"I'm sorry," her dad said. "The new one? It failed."

"But I saw the numbers. There are tons of views!" Annie was shocked.

"I'm sorry too," her mom said. "That we ever said okay."

Annie felt dizzy. Her heart raced. Her palms felt cold. She closed her eyes.

Do not cry, she told herself. *No matter what happens.*

She didn't want to be a baby. Not about this. It was a video. Spud wasn't dying.

Where was the dog? He was standing by his food bowl. "Come here," she told him. "We can take it. Whatever *it* is."

The dog trotted to her. She petted his head.

Dogs make everything better.

"Okay." Annie sat. Spud put his head on her lap. "Tell me what's up."

Her dad faced her. "Your video ..."

"It's not well liked," her mom said.

"To say the least," her dad added.

Annie dug her nails into her palms. "How bad is it?"

Her dad met her eyes. "The comments are okay. But the big guys think it's lame. They say it's too slick. Too produced. Too pro. They say you should quit."

Annie reached for the laptop. "Let me see."

Her mom shook her head. "Take our word for it. You don't want to read them." She banged the table with her palm. "It's not right. They're just kids."

Annie felt her voice go hollow. "They liked it better with the cell phone."

"I'm afraid that's true," her mom said.

Annie slumped in her chair. "But it was Big Don's idea. We didn't ask for a film crew!"

Her dad's phone sounded. He looked at it. "New York. I think it's Big Don."

"Get it," Annie told him. "Please, Dad."

He did. Her dad was right. It was the TV host. Her dad said hello. Then he gave her the phone. "He wants to talk to you."

Annie took it. She still felt sick. "Hi."

"Hi, Annie." Big Don spoke softly. "Look, I'm sorry. But we're going to have to put off the show. You know how it is. Give the public what they want," he said. "Anyway, stay in touch. And good luck."

Annie was not ready to click off. She had stuff to say.

"You know we didn't need the film crew," she told him. "We were fine how we were. Please let us do a new one. Our own way. Please?"

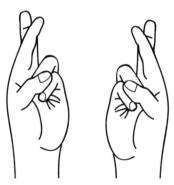

Big Don was silent for a second. Like maybe he'd say yes.

No.

"Sorry. It's a hard biz. Have a good life. See you later." He hung up.

Annie stared at her dad's phone. Big Don had said, *"Have a good life."* Like no one said, ever.

It didn't matter. What mattered was her dream was dead.

10
DOING GOOD

Annie met her friends before class. She'd texted them. Now they had the bad news too. It hurt. Randa's eyes were red. So were Tommy's.

She could tell they had been crying.

"I was all set for New York," he said.

"Maybe we can do one more," Erin said. "Use our phones. Do it our way. Like the first one."

Annie shook her head. She knew YouTube. You had one chance. That was it. People would find the next big thing. For a second, they were it. Now they were toast.

"I don't think so. Let's just go to class, guys."

That's what they did. It had been fun while it lasted.

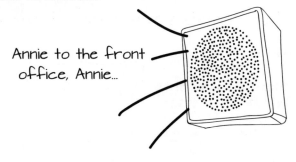

Annie to the front office, Annie...

Annie was in math when the call came. She had to go to the office. Dr. Marks wanted to see her. He was the principal. What did he want? Was she in trouble?

Dr. Marks smiled when she came in. "Hi,

Annie. I'm sorry about the Big Don show. It must feel bad."

"It does, yes. Thank you, Dr. Marks."

"You kids live in a fast new age. You can go from high to low like that." He snapped his fingers. "It may not be a good thing. We'll see."

"Yes, sir," she said. She wondered where this was going.

"Would you ever do your show again?"

Annie shook her head. "No way, sir. We're done. No more. We just want to get on with life."

"How about one more show? Just for the hospital kids. The head nurse called me. They want you. Can you do it for them?"

Annie gulped. She had said they were done. But …

"When?"

"Now. You can leave class. I've talked to your folks. It's all set up. Are you in?"

Annie was in. Randa, Tommy, and Erin were in the hallway. She talked to them. They were in too.

Spud and Candy are in too.

A van took Just Some Kids to the hospital.

It was a warm day. There was a stage out front. The clinic kids were on the grass.

The group sang "This Little Light of Mine." The kids loved it. Spud barked loudly. Candy mewed perfectly. Annie even got the kids to sing along. Being a star didn't matter. What mattered was doing good.

It had been a hard day. The song made it a lot better.

As she sang, Annie felt a little light inside her. It got bigger and bigger. She felt like it could light the world.